123 SESAME STREET

ONCE UPON A

SESAME STREET

CHRISTMAS

BASED ON THE SCRIPT BY GERI COLE, ADAPTED BY ROBIN NEWMAN
ILLUSTRATED BY TOM BRANNON

RP|KIDS
PHILADELPHIA

Sesame Workshop.® Sesame Street. ® and associated characters, trademarks and design elements are owned and licensed by Sesame Workshop. © 2017 by Sesame Workshop. All rights reserved.

Published by Running Press Kids,
An Imprint of Perseus Books, LLC,
A Subsidiary of Hachette Book Group, Inc.

Printed in China

ISBN 978-0-7624-6162-2
Library of Congress Control Number: 2016951728

9 8 7 6 5 4 3 2 1
Digit on the right indicates the number of this printing

Cover and interior design by Frances J. Soo Ping Chow
Edited by Karen Halpenny and Julie Matysik
Typography: Adobe Caslon and Wellfleet

Running Press Book Publishers
2300 Chestnut Street
Philadelphia, PA 19103–4371

Visit us on the web!
www.runningpress.com/rpkids
www.sesamestreet.org

It was Christmas Eve on Sesame Street
and everyone was full of holiday spirit!

"Elmo is so excited for Christmas!" Elmo said.
"Me, too!" said Abby.

"Me, three!" said Rosita.

"One, two, three monsters excited for Christmas," added the Count. "Ah, ah, ah!"

There was also one *not*-so-excited monster.

"Christmas is rotten! Cheerfulness? Gift giving? Bleh!" said Oscar the Grouch.

"What do grouches celebrate, then?" asked Abby.

"Crankymas. That's when we argue and give each other junk. It's the best!"

"Me like Christmas," said Cookie Monster. "Me can't wait for Santa
to come. Me love making cookies for Santa!"

At home that night, Elmo remembered to leave cookies out for Santa. Then he put on his jammies, brushed his teeth, and got all snuggled into bed.

When his daddy came to tuck him in, Elmo asked, "Daddy, why do we leave cookies out for Santa?"

"Well, Elmo, I'll tell you why. It's a good story. Once upon a Christmas Eve, Sesame Street was a very different place," he said. "There were no cars or electric lights. The people were different, too."

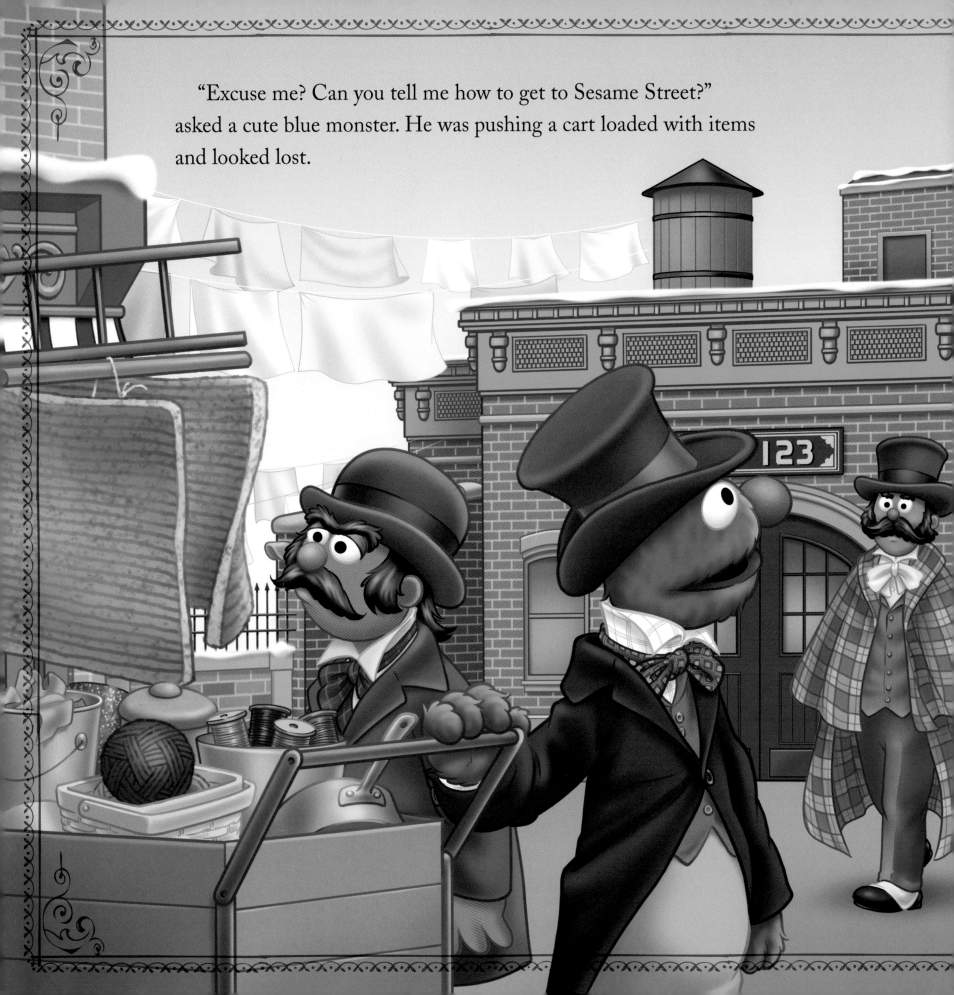

"Excuse me? Can you tell me how to get to Sesame Street?" asked a cute blue monster. He was pushing a cart loaded with items and looked lost.

No one stopped to answer except Oscar's great-great-grandgrouch, Oscar the Malcontent. "You're here. Now scram!" And Oscar was actually the *nicest* person on Sesame Street.

"Wait! Elmo doesn't understand. Oscar the Grouch was the nicest person on Sesame Street?"

"He was. Back then people weren't as kind to one another as they are now. Everyone was on Santa's naughty list."

"Daddy, is this a true story?" asked Elmo.

"It's just pretend. But you can still learn something from the story if you listen closely. Now, let's get back to Grover."

"Hello, customer," said Grover. "I'm selling handy-dandy welcome mats and . . ."

"BAM"

"My goodness! Why is everyone so rude?"

"Don't you know? Sesame Street is the unfriendliest street in town," said Constable Johnson as he walked by. "Why, bread doesn't like jam, two doesn't get along with three, grapes are sour, and even the crabs are super crabby!"

Suddenly, a wonderfully delicious smell wafted through the air.
It was the smell of cookies fresh out of the oven. Grover wondered
how the unfriendliest street could have such a friendly smell, so he
followed his nose.

"Hello there, baker! I would like two of your finest chocolate chippie cookies, please," said Grover.

"Sorry. Cookies all for me," said Cookie Monster. "None for you!" Then he gobbled up every last one!

That was the Christmas Eve your great-great grandmonster Elmo moved to 123 Sesame Street. He was just a little monster then, but he sure did love Christmas. He couldn't help noticing, however, that there were no Christmas decorations anywhere in sight.

"That's peculiar," his daddy said. "Maybe they hang them inside?"

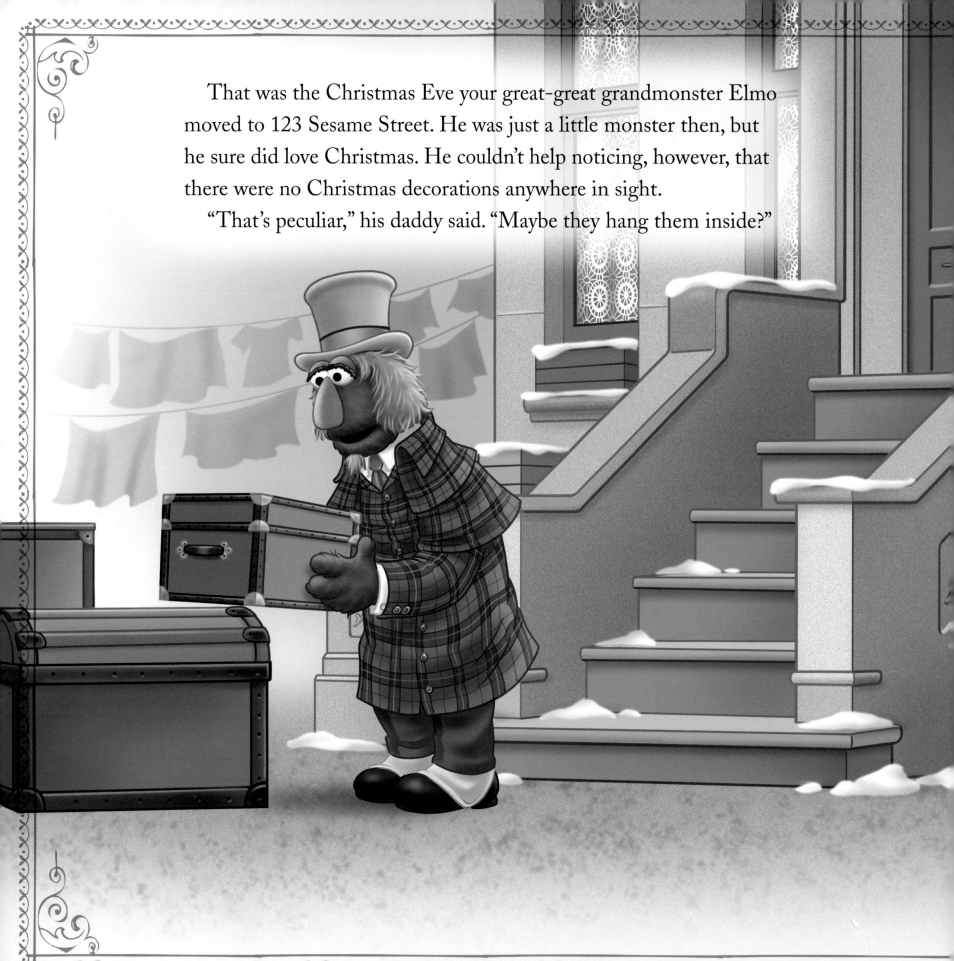

While Elmo's daddy unpacked, Elmo played with his favorite ball until it bounced away from him.

"Merry Christmas!" said Elmo to the girl who caught his ball.

"Merry Who-zits?" asked the girl. She had never heard of Christmas!

"May Elmo have his ball back?" Elmo asked.

"This is my ball!" the girl said.

"That's Elmo's ball. It has an 'E' on the side."

"That's not an 'E.' It's a smudge. . . . And that's *my* name. Smudge! So it's *my* ball!"

"Smudge, it's not nice to take someone else's ball. But Elmo would like someone to play with . . . and it is Christmas. So you can keep Elmo's ball, and we can play together!"

Out of nowhere, there was
a flash of light.
"What was that?" asked Elmo.
"What was what?" Smudge asked.
She hadn't seen it!

Elmo ran toward the light and came upon a funny little store called The Curiosity Shop. He opened the creaky door, stepped inside, and met Bella, the owner.

"Merry Christmas!" Elmo said.

"Merry Christmas, indeed!" shouted Bella. "Holly, this little monster can see us. He must have the holiday spirit."

"Who's Holly?" asked Elmo.

Bella pointed to the strange, clock-like object on the counter.

"I'm Holly the holiday spirit meter," it said. "The more people share the holiday spirit, the more I light up. If all five of my lights are lit, Santa will finally come to Sesame Street, just like we've always hoped."

"But how? It's already Christmas Eve!" Elmo said. "There isn't much time, but Elmo wants to help!"

Elmo ran outside to tell Smudge about Bella and Holly—and Santa coming to Sesame Street.

"Bella and Holly and Santa who?" she asked.

"There's no time!" Elmo said. "We need more holiday spirit!"

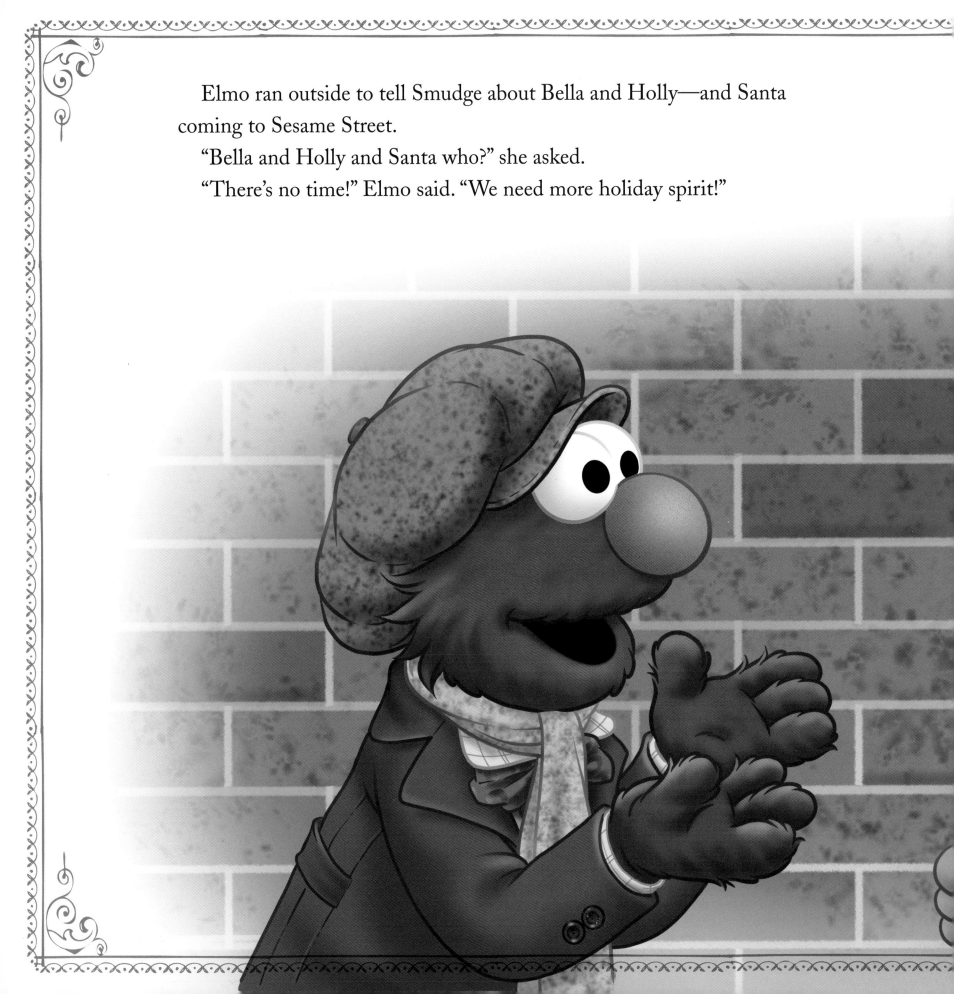

"You seem like a bright guy," said Smudge. "You shouldn't try to bring Christmas here. It'll never work."

"Bright! That's it. Decorations will brighten everything up," Elmo said. "And maybe that will give everyone enough holiday spirit for Santa to come!"

But Elmo didn't have any Christmas decorations.

Just then, Grover came along with his cart. "Curios! Bric-a-brac!"
he hollered.

"Elmo needs decorations to bring the holiday spirit to Sesame
Street. Do you have any for sale?" he asked.

Grover sold Elmo the decorations for a song, which they sang while
they decorated a nearby tree.

Santa flies tonight!
He'll be here before
you know it!
If you have some spirit,
Now's the time to show it.

"Yuck!" cried Oscar.

"Can I help?" asked Big Bird. "As I was on my way south, I spotted your decorations. I thought, *This must be a friendly place*."

"Sesame Street is the unfriendliest street. A fancy tree won't change that," said Smudge.

But it *was* changing. One of Holly's lights lit up!

"Decorations are nice," said Holly. "But it's not enough holiday spirit for Santa to come. Only one light is lit."

"We need more spirit," Bella said. "We need more kindness!"

Meanwhile, two traveling performers named Bert and Ernie were passing through and began to sing.

"No singing allowed!" shouted Constable Johnson.

"Elmo knows!" said Elmo. "A Christmas song will help bring holiday spirit to Sesame Street. And Elmo knows just what to do!"

Grover distracted Constable Johnson with big, fluffy earmuffs.
Bert, Ernie, and Elmo led everyone in singing "Deck the Halls."
Even Cookie Monster hummed along from his bakery window.

Just as the singing stopped, Constable Johnson pulled off his fluffy earmuffs. "Hey! Something strange is going on here!"

"Hmmm, I don't think so," Smudge said.

"Well, I'm feeling nice so I'll let you all go. Wait. Did I just do something *nice*?"

Bella noticed all of the happy faces.
"Something is definitely happening in town," she said. "Look at
Holly. She has three lights on!"

Suddenly, one light went out and there were only two left on.

"Santa's not coming, is he?" asked Smudge sadly.

"I'm afraid not," said Bella. "But you should still be very proud of what you've done."

Smudge tapped Elmo on the shoulder.

"Here's your ball back. I'm sorry I took it. Nobody's ever been kind to me before. Merry Christmas, Elmo."

"Merry Christmas, Smudge."

"Actually, my name's not Smudge. It's Becky."

"Well, then, Merry Christmas, Becky!" Elmo said, giving her a hug.

"Wait, Becky, that's it!
Decorations and singing
aren't enough to make
Holly's lights shine.
We need more kindness."

So Elmo and Becky started
being kind . . . and the kindness
started catching on.

"Look!" Big Bird pointed up at a sleigh in the sky.

"Santa!" said Elmo.

But there were only four lights lit up on Holly, so Santa's sleigh passed right by Sesame Street.

"We tried," said Becky. "At least Sesame Street is now the friendliest street in town."

Cookie Monster came around with a tray of cookies.

"Everyone being kind. Me try kindness! Me share cookies."

Suddenly, Holly's fifth light started blinking . . . and then it lit up all the way!

"One, two, three, four, five! Five festive lights," counted the Count.

"We did it!" cried Elmo.

But it was too late. Santa was already gone.

"Daddy, stop the story!" Elmo said. "It's not fair. They were all being so kind!"

"Don't worry, Elmo. The story's not over yet," his daddy assured him.

Just then, Santa saw a new street appear on his map.
"Well, look at this bright new light! Turn this sleigh around,"
he told his elf. "We're going to Sesame Street!"

When Santa landed, he wished everyone a Merry Christmas. "You were all so kind to each other, and had so much holiday spirit," Santa said. "I think I'll be coming back to Sesame Street every year!" Then he handed out presents to one and all.

Snow began to fall lightly just as Cookie Monster approached Santa with a plate of his favorite cookies.

"Me give cookies to Santa."

"A cookie? For me?" Santa took a big bite. "Mmm, delicious! I could get used to this!"

"And that is why we leave cookies for Santa, and that is how the holiday spirit came to Sesame Street," said his daddy.

"Merry Christmas, Elmo," whispered Santa.

"And Merry Christmas to all!"